CW00867367

ISBN: 978-1-69-513453-9

This book is dedicated to the memory of

William Ross Stuart

12/10/1939 – 13/01/2007

ACKNOWLEDGMENTS:

I'd like to thank the following; My wife, Suzanne for her encouragement, support and patience, my children, Michael, Benjamin & Cara, for their inspiration. Mike Faulkner, for his help in editing this book and finally, Lintang Pandu for her wonderful illustrations that brought Selkirk's Island to life.

Do you remember the time

Not that long ago

When you listened intently

To the stories of old

When each cliff-hanger

Made your heart skip a beat

And each chapter you read

Had you on the edge of your seat

Stories of monsters

And their innocent prey

Then along came the hero

To save the day

This story however is not about frights

It's a story of friendship and

Putting things right

Don't worry, there's a twist and cliff-hangers galore

With each chapter you read

You'll cry out for more

So enjoy, read on, let the story be told

Will you guess the twist?

Will you see it unfold……

Chapter 1

The old lady

It was another beautiful summer day. The sun had shone all morning and the only sound was the gentle tide, teasing the sand below. 'The song of the sea,' the old lady murmured, as she looked out from her garden at the yachts bobbing up and down on the waves.

Her thoughts were suddenly interrupted by footsteps coming up from the beach.

'Not more people ignoring the Private sign!' she sighed.

'Hello,' said the young man, climbing the last few steps. 'I hope you don't mind – my wife and I were walking along with the kids and realised we had run out of beach, so to speak. Would it be ok if we came up this way?'

The old lady peered over her glasses, sizing them up.

There was a commotion behind them and all of a sudden two children came bounding up the steps.

'Hi, I'm Paul,' announced the little boy with a wide smile. 'I'm six!'

'And I'm Emma,' said the girl standing beside him. 'I'm nine, and I'm his big sister.'

'Well, that's great news. I'll alert the press,' said the old lady.

Emma laughed.

'I'm sorry for interrupting your peace and quiet,' said the man. 'I'm Michael and this is my wife, Suzanne.'

'Hi there,' said Suzanne. 'We've just bought the house at the end, but we don't move in until next month. We're just here to find out as much as we can about the village before we move in.'

'Like the tide times?' said the old lady, with a cheeky smile.

'Yes,' said David, laughing. 'That might have been useful. We—'

'How long have you lived here?' Emma asked.

'Oh, it's been so long, I can hardly remember. I came here when I was nine and now ... well, now I'm a lot older.' She smiled. 'So yes, a very, very long time ago indeed!'

'You must know everything about here then?' said Paul.

The old lady turned to Paul.

'Not quite, dear,' she said, 'but there are things I could tell you about the bay that not many people know.'

'Can you tell us?' asked Emma.

'Please!' said Paul.

Suzanne interrupted.

'Let's not disturb the lady any more, children. I'm sure she has more important things to be getting on with!'

'It's okay,' said the old lady, 'I'll be glad to tell them something about the bay. There is one story that I've never told anyone.'

Michael looked over at Suzanne. 'Really?' he said. He looked at his watch. 'We're all ears.'

He sat down on the low wall that enclosed the garden, and patted the stone next to him, looking up at his wife. She hesitated for a moment, then joined him.

Paul and Emma were already sitting on the grass.

'Where to begin,' said the old lady. 'Where to begin ...'

'At the beginning!' said Paul.

Emma giggled.

'I'll tell the jokes!' said the old lady.

She leaned forward and began........

'It was a very long time ago. It all began one beautiful autumn morning. A little girl called Cara was about to waken up, not realising that this was the day her life would change forever...'

Chapter 2

Cara

The sun shone through a slight gap in the curtains.

Cara awoke to the sound of the local cockerel, crowing in the distance. She turned and looked over at her clock. It was twenty past eight.

Brilliant, she thought, and wrapped the pillow around her ears.

'Cara! If you're up, come downstairs. I've made some breakfast for you!'

'Are you joking, Dad? It's now precisely ... eight twenty-one. And it's Saturday!'

'Well, I just figured if you're awake, you might want to have breakfast with your old dad.'

'Okay, okay. I'll be down in a minute. Can I bring my blanket?'

'No!'

'Great! I'll just freeze then.'

'Put on your dressing gown. I've made a coal fire. It's roasting down here.'

She slowly slid out from under her blanket, stood up, grabbed her dressing gown and promptly fell backwards onto her bed.

I love my bed, she thought. *But he's not going to let up* ...

Cara jumped up, ran out of the bedroom, picked up the pillow she had left at the top of the stairs and slid on it all the way down to the bottom.

'Wheeeee!' she shouted as she bounced off the last step.

'Morning ... again,' said her dad as Cara came into the kitchen, rubbing her eyes.

'So, what's for breakfast?'

'Big fry-up. Bacon, sausages, eggs and beans.'

'Wow!' said Cara. 'What's the occasion?'

'I just thought it would be nice for a change.'

Cara wolfed it all down.

'Thanks Dad, that was great,' she said. 'I'm going to get ready, then I'm off to the beach. I need more shells for my school project. I'll see you in about an hour?'

'Okay. I've got something planned for lunch, so be back here at twelve. Yes?'

'Yep,' said Cara, but she was already halfway up the stairs, other things on her mind.

Running down the steps and onto the beach below, Cara was already looking left and right for the shells she needed. She had brought a small wicker basket to collect them in.

There wasn't a cloud in the sky. The tide was fully out and there was only the slightest whisper of a breeze. The sea, thought Cara, looked as if she could skate on it.

It was the small cockle shells she was looking for. The project was called, *Where I Live.* Each pupil could choose how they wanted to describe where they lived, and Cara had decided to use shells in a grand painting that would show the class all about life by the beach.

She started walking over a drift of seaweed left behind by the last tide. She loved to hear the popping sound it made. It always brought a smile to her face.

'Psssst!'

Cara looked around to see where the sound was coming from. She couldn't see anything, and continued looking for shells.

'Pssst. Psssssst!'

She looked up towards the bank, beyond the high tide mark, and there he was, sitting right on the edge of the beach – a rather plump-looking rabbit.

He had a straw hat on top of his head, with two holes cut out for his big floppy ears, and he was wearing torn grey shorts that went all the way down to just below his knees.

He was also holding, in a firm grip, a large wooden stick.

Cara shrieked!

Chapter 3

Selkirk

'Sit down here, next to me,' said the rabbit. 'The race is about to start!'

Cara, still wondering what was going on, rather hesitantly did as she was told and sat down on some dry, crunchy seaweed next to the rabbit.

'You're t-t-talking!' said Cara.

'So are you.'

'But I'm a girl.'

'And I'm a rabbit. My name is Selkirk. What's yours?'

'It's Cara,' replied Cara.

'That's an odd name,' said Selkirk, and chuckled.

'Were you born in a Caravan?' he asked. He was laughing now. 'Get it?' Cara, Cara - van! Ha-ha!'

'Yeah, you should be a comedian,' said Cara. *He's about as funny as two hours of maths*, she thought to herself.

As they were talking, a large number of birds, of all shapes and sizes, had begun to gather on the beach.

'Look!' said Selkirk, pointing up to the sky. 'King Markus Theodore is about to start the race.'

'Of course he is,' said Cara with a smirk.

King Markus Theodore, Selkirk explained, had flown years ago from his native Brazil, all the way across the Atlantic Ocean, in a quest to find his long-lost relatives in Portugal.

'He has always claimed to have been blown off course, but between you and me' – he tapped his stick against the side of his nose, and winked – 'I think he may have got lost.'

King Markus had since settled in the bay and was now regarded as part of the big family of birds and animals.

Above them, perched on a branch of the ancient oak tree that stretched out over the foreshore, stood the majestic figure of King Markus Theodore the Third. Very regal indeed, thought Cara, his green, red and yellow plumage surpassed only by his crown of blue feathers.

He truly was a handsome parrot.

King Markus Theodore flapped his wings and announced to the now silent crowd:

'I, King Markus Theodore the Third, ruler of all Amazonia, do hereby declare the 75th Annual Largo Bay Race can now begin!'

Selkirk kept up a running commentary. Two birds stood side by side on the shingle of the island foreshore. The Seagulls, as usual, had entered their fastest bird in the race, a large and wide-winged gull by the name of Angus. He had won the race every year for the last nine years and was odds-on favourite for ten in a row.

The other bird was a magpie called Mikey. He was a young bird and had replaced Maggie, injured the previous day after a clumsy landing in the great oak tree.

Mikey was very inexperienced and, according to Selkirk, was clearly nervous – earlier, he had seen beads of sweat run from Mikey's forehead and down his beak. He flapped his impressive wings and puffed out his chest; clearly, he fully understood the size of the task ahead.

Selkirk looked out across the bay, towards the little hump-backed island with a clump of trees at its highest point. A rocky causeway, already partly submerged by the incoming tide, joined the island to the mainland.

'The start is on the island foreshore, opposite that enormous jagged boulder. They have to go once around the island before climbing to the top of the tallest tree on the hill.'

He pointed with his stick towards an ancient Scots pine, its canopy silhouetted against the sky.

'Then they cross to the mainland to pick up their twigs from the oak tree. A brown twig for Mikey and a black one for Angus. From there, they fly under the old railway bridge, before banking hard and swooping back, over the bridge this time, over the harbour and back to the island.

The first bird to successfully drop their twig in the basket on top of the hill wins. Old Olly, the owl, referees the whole thing. He's very good. Never misses a trick. Unfortunately, he wasn't here when the gulls won the island from us, but that's another story ...'

Cara looked puzzled.

'You mean the island belongs to you?' she said.

'It used to,' said Selkirk. 'The gulls cheated us out of it many, many years ago. There was never any proof, though, and so we just had to accept the decision.'

'That's terrible,' said Cara.

Just then a large heron flew high overhead, before swooping down towards the island.

'That's Henry,' said Selkirk.

As Henry landed on the jagged rock, he spread his gigantic wings and turned to face, first the Seagulls gathered on the island's shingly foreshore, then the crowd on the beach.

There was a sudden hush.

Henry paused for a second or two, enjoying the moment.

He then gave his usual high-pitched squawk, and the race began ...

Chapter 4

The race

Mikey got off to a great start, sending a little shower of pebbles behind him as he launched himself into the air.

There was very little in it by the time they had flown around the island.

Angus was right behind Mikey as they headed for the oak tree on the edge of the beach.

Below the two competitors, dozens of spectators – birds, foxes, rabbits and even Sammy and Selina, the two resident seals – all looked skywards, craning their necks to get the best view.

Both Mikey and Angus had chosen to gain height as they neared the oak tree, and as they circled above it, they were neck and neck, each bird getting his bearings and preparing his approach.

It was Mikey, however, who swooped down first on to the branch where his brown twig lay.

On his first attempt, he overshot the twig, slipped on the branch and went skidding along its full length, coming to a rather abrupt stop as he smashed into the thick trunk.

Angus, on the other hand, with so much more experience, glided gently down, picked up his black twig and without even a pause, continued his flight towards the old railway bridge.

There were shrieks all around from down below when Mikey came to an abrupt halt. He almost had to peel himself off the trunk and as he turned around, a single downy feather drifted to the ground.

The brown twig was still there though.

'All is not lost,' he mumbled, as he picked it up and hoisted his now weary body back into the air.

He could see in the distance Angus flying low as he approached the bridge. If he could just pick up some speed, he might be able to catch him.

As Mikey approached the bridge, Angus had already made his turn and was on his way back over it.

Mikey's turn wasn't exactly elegant, and he appeared to skid in the sky, slipping sideways.

He kept going and going, until finally he came to a shuddering halt against the branch of an old apple tree. He fell to the ground in a heap and tried to compose himself. Just as he was about to fly off again, a single apple dislodged itself and came crashing down on his head ...

'Ouch!'

Angus was now back over the old railway bridge and he even had time to look back at Mikey.

But Mikey was now too far back, and although he took to the air and kept flying gamely on, Angus was already beyond the harbour wall and racing towards the island.

Mikey knew he had blown it.

Angus knew it too as he reached the island, fully half a minute ahead of his plucky rival.

Mikey was starting to tire, but gave it one last push.

Onwards and upwards! he thought.

As Mikey flew over the island foreshore, Angus was just a few short feet from the basket.

Olly the owl, watching from above, knew it was all over.

As predicted, earlier, by Angus himself ... He certainly wasn't the most modest seagull who ever took to the air.

He won easily, dropping his twig into the basket.

A loud roar went up from all of the gulls on the island, while the mainland crowd fell silent.

Mikey flew slowly and sadly back to the great oak tree.

On a branch near the top, looking down, stood King Markus Theodore the Third.

'Don't worry son, you tried your very best,' said King Markus Theodore.

'I blew it!' said Mikey.

'There's always next year,' said King Markus Theodore. 'Don't be sad. You're young. You just need a bit of training. You got so close ...'

'By next year, Maggie will be back. I've lost my chance,' said Mikey.

King Markus Theodore draped his ample wing around Mikey's shoulders and said, 'You'll get your chance again, I'm sure of it.'

The beach and the dunes, where just a few minutes ago stood hundreds of hopeful animals, were now almost deserted.

They had all gone back to their trees and bushes, their burrows, the sea.

Side by side in sullen silence, sat Cara and Selkirk.

After several minutes, Selkirk said quietly, 'Well, that's us lost again.'

He looked over to the island. The Seagulls, once again the victors, were celebrating wildly by flapping their wings, squawking and cheering.

Angus was being hailed a hero for the tenth year in a row.

'Mikey did his best,' said Cara.

'I know,' said Selkirk, 'but it just wasn't good enough!'

Chapter 5

Robert McRabbie

'Tell me how you lost the island,' said Cara.

'You really want to know?'

'Of course.'

'Well, it was a very long time ago,' said Selkirk. 'I need to take you right back to the very beginning. To an ancestor of mine, a rabbit named Robert McRabbie. Well, one day—'

'Robert McRabbie? Was that his real name?'

'Yes,' said Selkirk. 'It's a perfectly normal name!'

'Okay,' said Cara, trying to stifle a laugh.

'Right, where was I?' said Selkirk.

'Your ancestor, Robert McRabbie? Cara smiled.

'Oh yes,' said Selkirk. 'Well, one day when Robert was quite young, he heard that a shipment of carrots was coming in on a merchant boat down at the harbour. He got down there early and waited. When the ship arrived, he sneaked aboard. Eventually he found the boxes of carrots, but there were a lot of sailors around. So, he decided to wait until they all went ashore to the tavern.

'Once they had all left, Robert climbed on top of one of the boxes and managed to prise it open. He couldn't believe it, there were thousands and thousands of carrots. He'd hit the jackpot!

'Just as Robert was about to lift some carrots out of the box, he heard the door of the ship's galley creak open. As he turned to look, he lost his balance and promptly fell into the open box!

Whoever had come in had now left – Robert could hear the door close. Unfortunately for Robert, it was a very deep box and he could barely move, never mind climb out!

'All of a sudden, Robert heard the sound of the giant anchor being pulled up. The ship was about to leave and Robert was well and truly stuck!'

'Ok, let me just stop you there!' said Cara. 'I need to get this straight.'

'So, you're telling me, first of all, and let me get his name right ... Robert McRabbie' – she was now chuckling – 'tried to steal some carrots from on board a ship' – now she was laughing out loud – 'but fell into the box, couldn't get out and was now adrift at sea with thousands of carrots!?'

The tears of laughter were now rolling down Cara's cheeks.

'Okay, okay!' said Selkirk. 'Calm down! It's not that funny. Now, do you want to hear the rest of the story or not?'

'I'm sorry,' said Cara, still smiling. 'Please, carry on ...'

'Very well,' said Selkirk. 'Have you heard of the famous Scottish sailor, Alexander Selkirk?'

'Yes, of course,' said Cara. 'He was born here. He was also marooned on an island for a while many years ago. Most people know him as Robinson Crusoe. There's a statue of him down in the village.'

'That's correct,' said Selkirk. 'There's also a statue of Robert on the island. The woodpeckers made it.

'Anyway, it just so happens that Alexander Selkirk was aboard the ship. And unfortunately for Robert, it was heading for South America! During the voyage, Alexander found Robert down in the galley.

He very quickly realised that this was no ordinary rabbit, as he could, well ... speak.

'So, they became friends and when Alexander asked to be put ashore on the island of Juan Fernandez near Chile, Robert went with him.'

'Why did Alexander ask to be put ashore?' asked Cara.

'He had decided,' replied Selkirk, 'that the ship was no longer seaworthy and that it might sink!

'He took Robert with him, expecting to be picked up by another ship within a few days. Unfortunately, that didn't happen for quite some time. Alexander and Robert made a life for themselves on the island and became experts in hunting and foraging'

'They also found a waterfall with fresh water. They had everything they needed. It took over four years for them to be rescued! On the way back, they parted company in England and Robert eventually found his way home, to Largo Bay. He decided to make a home for himself and his family on the island. And in honour of his famous friend, he decided to call it Selkirk's Island'

'In due course, more animals came to live on the island and they all lived very happily together. When Robert's first son was born, he decided to name him after his friend Alexander Selkirk'

'A tradition that still continues to this day.'

Chapter 6

'The race was fixed!'

'Wow!' said Cara. 'But you've still not explained how you lost the island to the gulls?'

'I'm getting to that,' said Selkirk. 'For many years the Seagulls were the sworn enemies of all other birds and animals that lived in and around the bay, due to the fact that they were always stealing food and fighting.'

'Long after Robert died, my great-grandfather, also called Selkirk and now head of the island, was approached by the King of the Seagulls, a huge gull called King Steven who suggested a way of ending their feud.

'He suggested that they have a race between one of his flock and any bird that my great-grandfather wanted to race on his herd's behalf.

'King Steven said that if my great-grandfather's nominated bird won then they, the Seagulls, would leave the bay for good, never to return. However, if the Seagulls won, then my great-grandfather would be forced off the island and it would become home to all of King Steven's flock.

'Well, my great-grandfather thought long and hard about this and after consulting with the island's elders, decided that he couldn't possibly lose as long as he could persuade the fastest bird to race.

'That bird was, and still is to this day, considered the most famous racer of Largo Bay's history. His name was Micah "The Meteor" Magpie.

'Micah agreed to race for the honour of the island, and on the day of the race he was in perfect condition and full of confidence,' said Selkirk. "'I won't let you down!" he assured my great-grandfather.

'On the gull's side was an unusually large seagull called Hector. Hector had been training for weeks before the race and had been telling anyone who would listen that he was going to coast to victory.

'Micah got off to a great start as expected. However, half way around, his left wing suddenly stopped flapping! Down below, in the crowd of spectators, no one could understand what was wrong ...

'Well, to cut a long story short,' said Selkirk, 'Micah lost. His wing had been broken and he fell into the harbour. Hector won comfortably and became the hero of the gulls. 'The gulls wasted no time at all and took over the island, forcing my great-grandfather onto the beach between the high and low water mark. For a long time after, there were rumours that the race had been fixed and that someone on the gull's side had thrown something at Micah, which hit his wing.

'No one knew for sure,' said Selkirk. 'There was no proof. The island was lost and eventually Micah flew off, never to be seen again! The rabbits, foxes and all the rest of the birds and animals made their home on the beach and in the trees.

'And now the race is run every year, just for fun,' said Selkirk.

Cara looked at the sadness in Selkirk's eyes and said, 'Have you ever tried to get the island back?'

'No,' said Selkirk. 'No one could ever find the proof and the Seagulls have never talked about it either. It's a lost cause.'

'Well, there must be proof somewhere,' said Cara.

'I'm sure there is. But where?'

Cara looked over at the island.

The tide was coming in.

'I have an idea,' said Cara, grinning. 'Let's start over there.' She pointed at the island. 'That's where we'll find the proof!'

'Great! But how do we get there? The tide is almost fully in,' said Selkirk. 'We can't use the rocks and I can't swim!'

'What time is it?' asked Cara.

'Do I look like a clock?' said Selkirk. 'The sun is at its highest … so, it must be around midday. Why?'

'I need to be home,' said Cara. 'My dad is making me lunch.'

'Lucky you!' said Selkirk. 'I've just got this old dirty carrot!'

'Meet me here later, when the moon comes up,' said Cara. 'Don't be late. I have a plan!'

She gave Selkirk a hug before running all the way back to the house.

Chapter 7

The plan

When Cara arrived home, her dad was in the kitchen making lunch.

Sat beside him was Holly, their beautiful golden retriever.

'Dad! You won't believe what just happened to me!'

As Cara finished her sentence she looked down at Holly, who seemed to be shaking her head.

Oh, thought Cara. *Is she saying, 'Don't tell him'? She is*!

Holly was still shaking her head when Dad said, 'Yes Cara, what is it, what happened?'

'Em, er, never mind Dad, it's n-not important. I'm just going upstairs to wash my hands for lunch. I'll be down in a minute.'

Cara washed her hands and then came bounding down the stairs and into the kitchen.

'What's for lunch?' she asked.

'Pasta with chicken – your favourite,' said Dad.

'Great!'

'Did you get the shells you were looking for?' asked Dad.

Cara looked at Holly, who appeared to be smiling at her. Possibly in anticipation of how Cara was about to explain how she came back with no shells, and no basket either ...

'There weren't a lot of shells on the beach today, Dad,' she said.

Holly barked!

'Shhh!' Cara raised her finger and gave Holly a hard stare. 'The tide must have taken most of them,' she said, winking at Holly. 'I'll get the rest tomorrow.'

'No shells? On a beach? Well that's a first!' said Dad, not really paying that much attention as he continued stirring the chicken into the pasta.

Cara ate all of her pasta up at record speed.

'I think I'll go and do some homework now, Dad,' she said. 'It's due in for Monday.'

'Okay,' said Dad. 'I'm going to take Holly out for a walk.'

Cara went up the stairs and into her room. She felt a little bit guilty for not telling her dad the truth.

But I just can't tell him, she thought. *And I must help Selkirk!*

Cara stretched out on her bed, going over in her head the plan she had thought would work best.

But she was so tired. Maybe it was the sea air and all the excitement, maybe it was the big portion of pasta. Who knew? But whatever it was, and without her even realising, she promptly fell asleep...

Cara was asleep for a whole three hours, and woke up startled.

Was it all just a dream? she thought.

No! It was all very real.

Cara hadn't noticed, but Holly had crept into her room whilst she was sleeping and was sitting there staring at her.

It looked again like Holly was trying to say something. But she just barked.

'For a minute there, I thought you were going to talk,' said Cara.

Now Holly looked like she was smiling.

Right! thought Cara. *I need to get organised, I can't be late for Selkirk!*

Two hours later, the sun started its usual evening descent behind the horizon. It was slowly getting dark.

The moon will be up soon, thought Cara. *Full moon, too.*

It was indeed a full moon, in a clear sky lit by a vast array of bright, sparkling stars.

Cara always marvelled at the sky on nights like this. She had studied a bit about space and the planets at school and knew of Orion's belt and the Plough amongst others. Tonight, though, wasn't a night for stargazing.

Tonight was all about helping Selkirk find the proof that would get the island back!

Now all Cara needed to do was to get out of the house without her dad knowing. She waited until his favourite programme came on the television. She had told him she was going to finish her homework and then go straight to sleep.

'That's great,' said her dad. 'Good night then, and I'll see you in the morning.'

Earlier, Cara had taken some of her dad's old rope out of the garden shed. She tied one end to her bed, dropped the rest out of the bedroom window, and now she was ready to climb down. She opened the window very slowly and quietly climbed onto the windowsill.

Just as she was about to go out of the window, Holly came into the bedroom.

She barked quite loudly.

'Shhhh!' said Cara. 'Dad will hear!'

As Cara started her descent down the rope, Holly's big face appeared at the window. She must have climbed onto Cara's bed.

Cara looked up at Holly's big beautiful face and just as she was about to slide down the last part of the rope, it happened again – Holly appeared to smile.

'Be careful,' said Holly.

Chapter 8

Benny the fox

Cara finally had her feet on solid ground.

So, Holly can speak after all! she thought, as she quietly tiptoed down the stony path next to the house, fearful that her dad might hear her footsteps.

She then ran across the soft grass, down the steps and onto the beach.

As she reached the great oak tree, she looked all around for Selkirk. He was nowhere to be seen.

She looked up into the sky. The full moon had risen high, more stars were appearing all around, but there was no sign of Selkirk.

Just then, out from behind the great oak tree bounced Selkirk.

'Boo!'

'That's not funny!' said Cara.

'I thought it was.' Selkirk laughed.

'Oh, I forgot,' said Cara. 'You're a comedian ...'

'Okay,' said Selkirk, 'no need for sarcasm. It was just a joke. Anyway, you're late!'

'I think you'll find I'm bang on time!' said Cara. 'Check your moon clock! Ha!

So, what's the plan?'

'Quite simple really,' said Cara. 'You and I are going over to the island!'

'Are you crazy!? Have you been drinking?'

'I'm eleven,' said Cara. 'Of course I haven't been drinking. Right! Here's the plan. We are going to row across in my dad's dinghy. It's pulled up on the beach just in front of our house. The tide is just about fully in and the gulls will all be sleeping'

'When we get there, we'll tie up the dinghy and look for evidence. Once we find it, we'll row back. What do you think?'

'I think I need a drink!' said Selkirk.

'We'll be fine! I've been out in the dinghy loads of times.'

'Great!' said Selkirk. 'Just give me a minute, so I can write my will …'

'Don't be daft,' said Cara. 'Now c'mon, let's go! We don't have much time!'

Just as they both set off along the beach, down swooped Mikey, the magpie.

'Hi,' said Mikey. 'I was listening in on your chat and I've decided I'd like to come too. I want to help!'

Cara looked over at Selkirk. He was now munching on a large carrot.

'Are you okay with that, Selkirk?' asked Cara.

'The more the merrier.'

At that moment, Benny the fox came scampering down the dunes.

'This is Benny,' said Selkirk to Cara.

'Hi,' said Cara. 'Pleased to meet you.'

'Likewise, doll face,' said Benny. 'I heard you cats were planning a little mission to Gull Island.'

'It's Selkirk's Island!' said Selkirk.

'Whatever, man, I just thought you cats could use my unique talents and martial arts skills.'

Benny was an odd character indeed. He certainly looked like a fox although he was wearing sunglasses and the whiskers on his snout made him look almost like he had a goatee beard.

Unusual, to say the least, thought Cara. But she instantly liked him.

Benny proceeded to demonstrate his martial arts skills, crashing his forearm down in a karate chop onto a piece of driftwood.

Thwack! It didn't break!

'Ouch!' screamed Benny.

'Well, that didn't go to plan,' said Mikey.

'Hey kid,' said Benny, 'it worked before. Have you seen my karate kick?'

Without waiting for an answer, Benny threw his leg in a sideways movement against another piece of driftwood, perched against the rocks.

'Aaaargh!'

'Right! Enough of all this nonsense!' said Cara. 'If you're coming, and if you can walk' – she looked at Benny – 'we need to go now!'

'Okay,' they said in unison and off they walked, flew – hobbled – along the beach to the dinghy.

Cara and Benny jumped into the dinghy first, whilst Mikey perched at the bow. Selkirk, however, was looking distinctly nervous as he stood, now alone, on the beach.

'What's the matter?' said Cara.

'Hey!' said Benny to Selkirk. 'I didn't think you were a scaredy cat!'

'I'm not!' said Selkirk. 'It's just that I've never been on a boat before. We used to get to the island by climbing over the rocks when the tide was out. Never this way!'

'You'll be fine.' Cara tried to sound reassuring. 'Now, get on board!'

'Aye aye Captain,' said Selkirk. He carefully stepped into the dinghy and settled himself at the stern.

Mikey perched on one of the oars, and as Cara rowed, he began to sway to and fro, flapping his wings now and then to keep his balance.

The moon was shining down on the island, lighting their way for the short trip across the bay.

It was very quiet when they arrived, and Cara dropped the dinghy's anchor in the shallows.

'Now,' she said. 'We all have to be deadly quiet, not a sound.'

Mikey opened his beak wide, threw his head back and closed his eyes.

'Aaaaa ... choo!'

'Are you guys for real?' said Cara. 'I've got a sneezing magpie, a scared stiff rabbit who can't stop shaking, and a fox who thinks he's a black belt at karate! Get your act together and follow me.'

She climbed out of the dinghy and onto the rocks. 'Remember, be quiet!'

Selkirk, Mikey and Benny all looked at each other and understood. Cara was in charge here!

They walked through some trees and into a clearing. There were lots of beautiful flowers, palm trees, oak trees, brightly coloured bushes, all with different textures, shapes and smells.

They kept walking, arriving at an area where there was a small pond surrounded by rocks and trees.

'Over there,' said Cara, pointing to a small hill. 'There is a cave just at the base of the hill. Let's go.'

Selkirk and Benny, without even realising, were now holding hands. It was Benny who spotted it first.

'Jeez Louise!' said Benny. 'What ya doin' man?!'

'What do you mean?' said Selkirk, and looked down at their clasped hands. 'Aagh!' he screamed, quickly pulling away.

'Don't do that again,' said Benny.

'Will you guys keep it down!' ordered Cara, and they continued up a slight incline towards the cave.

'How are we going to see in there?' said Mikey as they arrived at the entrance to the cave.

'Don't worry,' said Cara, and she pulled out a torch from her rucksack and promptly lit it with some matches. It flared into life. Ahead of them, the narrow path became visible in the darkness.

'Cool,' said Benny.

'I don't suppose you've got any carrots in there?' asked Selkirk.

Cara shot Selkirk a look and said, 'Does this look like a picnic!?'

'Sorry,' said Selkirk.

Benny and Mikey were quietly laughing.

'Shhhh!' said Cara.

In they went.

It was pitch black!

Cara shone the torch light slowly around the walls, glistening with water.

They all saw it together …

Chapter 9

The proof!

There in the beam of the torch, for all to see, were a series of paintings, and they appeared to show exactly what happened during that fateful race.

One of the paintings depicted a small seagull with what appeared to be a catapult, and he or she was aiming it at a bird flying above – a bird with the distinct close-coupled wings and long, diamond-shaped tail of a magpie.

It was Micah!

The next painting showed Micah being hit on the wing, and was followed by another showing him crashing into the harbour.

The final painting appeared to show King Steven placing a medal around the neck of the small gull.

'So, it was all true!' said Cara.

Selkirk nodded, and he gripped his stick tightly until the knuckles showed white in the torchlight. 'I knew it! The gulls planned the whole thing. It was a set-up from start to finish ... They couldn't lose!'

'It's clear as day. They fixed the race,' said Cara.

Mikey and Benny looked on.

'This is the ultimate crime indeed!' declared Benny.

'You're right!' said Mikey. 'We have to do something about this!'

'But what can we do?' said Selkirk. 'They'll just deny it, won't they?'

'They would if we approached the King right now ...' said Cara. She was silent for a moment. 'I have an idea,' she said. 'But first, we need to get off the island and back to shore. Let's go!'

As quietly as they could, they all crept out of the cave, down the slope, past the pond and across the clearing to the trees by the rocky beach where the dinghy was anchored.

Selkirk was first to speak as they approached the dinghy.

'If I could get my hands on the King, I'd ...'

'Now, now,' said Cara. 'There are other ways. We shouldn't stoop to their level.'

'I know,' said Selkirk, 'but I'm just so angry!'

'I know, and I can't blame you. But I have a plan.'

Before Cara could say anything else, a flapping sound came from the trees behind them.

'Run!' shouted Cara.

They all ran as fast as they could. Except Mikey, who flew. He was already perched on the end of one of the oars when the others arrived.

No one looked back. If they had, they would have seen King Steven glaring at them, his face and beak turning redder by the second, quivering with rage.

They were all in the dinghy now. Cara lifted the small anchor and started to row.

'Row like the clappers!' shouted Benny.

And she did!

A few minutes later, they reached the shore. The tide was starting to go out now, but there was just enough water to berth the dinghy in the same spot as before.

Very much out of breath, and somewhat shaken, they exchanged nervous smiles.

'We did it!' said Selkirk. 'What now?'

Cara looked at him, a glint of determination in her eye.

'What now? I'll tell you what now. Meet me here tomorrow when the sun is at its highest. Bring everyone from the woods, the trees, the sea – the burrows. Bring them all. Tomorrow, we march to the island!'

Chapter 10

The rope

The next morning Cara awoke, as usual, to the sound of the cockerel.

No need for an alarm clock here! she thought, as she stretched and climbed out of bed.

Cara peered out of her curtains. It was another beautiful morning, sunny and bright.

When she arrived downstairs, her dad was in the kitchen, making coffee for himself on the stove.

'What's for breakfast?' asked Cara.

'Toast,' said Dad.

'What! no fry-up?' said Cara, and pouted.

'Nope,' said Dad. 'It's toast or cornflakes.
And don't give me that look, Cara!'

'Okay, I'll have some toast, said Cara.

'Did you have a good sleep? Your light was
out awful early.'

'Yes, I d-did,' said Cara nervously,
wondering whether her dad was suspicious.

He obviously wasn't, though, as he didn't
say any more.

Holly looked up at Cara and barked.

'What is it Holly?' said Cara.

'Oh, she'll just be looking for another
biscuit,' said Dad. 'Ignore her.'

Holly was looking out the window at
something.

'What are you ...' Cara went to the window
and looked out. She gasped.

'What is it?' said Dad.

'Nothing,' gulped Cara. The rope was still dangling down from her bedroom window! 'I forgot my dressing gown. I'll be back in a minute.'

She raced up the stairs to her bedroom, jumped onto her bed, opened the window and grabbed the rope. She pulled it up gently and quietly, hoping that Dad wouldn't notice. Then she grabbed her dressing gown and ran back downstairs, jumping the last two steps.

'That was quick!' said Dad. 'Here's your toast.'

Phew!

After gulping down some milk, Cara went back up the stairs to get ready.

She had a big day ahead.

When she came back down the stairs and into the living room, her dad was stoking the fire. It sparked a little and Holly jumped off the sofa and ran into the hall.

'So, what's the plan today?' asked Dad.

'I think I'll go back onto the beach and see if I can find the shells I didn't get yesterday for my school project.'

'Well, don't be too long, your cousin Ellie is coming over today, remember?'

'I remember,' said Cara. 'What time is she coming?'

'About three o'clock.'

'Okay, I'll definitely be back by then. What time is it just now?'

'Just gone midday.'

'Okay. Better go. I'll see you later Dad. Bye!'

Cara ran out the house and down the steps onto the beach.

There was no sign of Selkirk, or anyone for that matter. She looked all around. Nothing.

Just as Cara was about to turn back, out they came ...

Chapter 11

March to the island

There were hundreds of them!

Out from behind the rocks and down from the trees behind Cara, came rabbits, foxes, stoats, hedgehogs, squirrels and so many different species of birds. There were gannets, puffins, magpies, cormorants, herons and even the albatross.

She lost count of how many animals and birds now faced her on the beach, but there must have been at least two hundred.

There, at the head of them all, was Selkirk. And standing proudly beside him were Mikey, Benny, Henry, Olly and of course King Markus Theodore, the Third.

Cara noticed another rabbit standing just behind Selkirk. Clearly a girl rabbit.

Cara stood on the big rock to get a better look at everyone, and Selkirk came up to her.

'What do you think?' he said.

'Fantastic!' said Cara. 'What a brilliant turnout. King Steven won't know what's hit him, so to speak.'

'Well, you did say bring everyone.' Selkirk chuckled.

'I did,' said Cara. 'But who's the girl rabbit that was standing behind you?'

Selkirk's cheeks went a bit red.

'That's Robin,' said Selkirk.

'Is she your girlfriend?'

'She's j-just a friend.'

Cara laughed. 'You should ask her out, if you haven't already.'

'Maybe one day,' said Selkirk, and blushed again. 'So! Can we get on with this? What's the plan?'

Cara told Selkirk the plan as they all marched over the rocky causeway to the island.

Behind them, Benny the fox was chatting to his friend Felix.

'Lucky the tide is out this time,' he said to Felix. 'Last night, when it was fully in, we had to row out!'

'Lucky you're a good rower!' said Felix.

'You're right there, man,' said Benny. This was no time to admit that Cara had done the rowing.

When they reached the island, the first thing they saw was the statue of old Robert McRabbie, right at the end of the causeway.

A magnificent sight it was indeed!

It had been fashioned by the woodpeckers many years ago, from what was left of an old tree. They had left the bottom three feet as a base and carved the image of Robert McRabbie above, with his hat and long shorts, holding his stick.

He looked just like Selkirk, Cara thought.

'The Seagulls at least respected his statue,' said Selkirk to Cara.

'Maybe they're not all bad then,' said Cara.

Just then, about a hundred seagulls flew out from the trees and swooped down. They very quickly formed a thick wall between Selkirk and Cara, and the rest of the island.

One of them then stepped forward.

'My name is Prince Sebastian,' he announced. 'What is the meaning of this? You are trespassing on our island!'

Chapter 12

King Steven

Selkirk stepped forward. Everyone was completely silent.

'We are here to speak to your father, King Steven,' said Selkirk. 'In fact, we demand an audience with him!'

'And who are you to demand anything?' said Prince Sebastian.

'My name is Selkirk and these are my friends.'

'You have a lot of friends!' said the Prince. 'You must be his descendant?' He pointed to the statue of Robert McRabbie.

'I am,' said Selkirk. 'My full title is Selkirk McRabbie the Eighth. I am the great-grandson of Selkirk McRabbie the Fifth.

'And what do you want of my father?' said the Prince.

'Just a private conversation, if that's not too much to ask?' said Selkirk.

Another Seagull flew up from behind the wall of gulls and landed at the feet of Prince Sebastian, whispering something in his ear.

Without warning, the Prince stepped back and the wall of gulls parted, creating a pathway to the hill behind them.

'We're in,' whispered Cara to Selkirk as they all walked between the two walls of gulls on either side of them.

As they approached the hill, King Steven appeared.

He was a giant of a gull and very frightening indeed.

'Why are you here, Selkirk?' said the King. 'You know this is our island and you're not welcome here!'

Selkirk took a deep breath.

'You stole this island from my great-grandfather! And you know it!'

The King roared with laughter.

'You are a funny little rabbit, aren't you!' he said. 'You have no proof!' He made a sweeping gesture with his wing. 'Come on! Where is your evidence?'

'Right behind you!' said Selkirk. 'In the cave at the foot of the hill. The paintings there are our proof!'

'There are no paintings in there,' said the King, laughing.

'Well let's all just go in and have a look, shall we?' said Selkirk. 'I'm sure we can clear this all up in a matter of minutes.'

Selkirk waved at the army of animals and birds behind him, gesturing them all to move forward.

'Wait a minute!' said the King, sweating now. He glanced at his sidekick and said under his breath, 'There are too many of them. We're outnumbered.'

Just then, another somewhat smaller gull came flying down, landing next to King Steven.

It was the Queen!

She looked angry, but surprisingly her anger seemed to be reserved for the King and not Selkirk.

She whispered something in his ear. The King appeared to redden, but more in embarrassment than anger.

The Queen flew off and King Steven turned to the assembled crowd.

'I admit,' he began, 'that there were perhaps some failings on our part during the race all those years ago.'

'Duh! Ya think?' mumbled Benny.

The King cleared his throat and continued..

'There maybe, could be, potentially, and don't quote me on this, perhaps some small amount of evidence in the cave, suggesting that, in theory, there is a slight chance that the race itself was not exactly – and I'm not taking the blame here, you understand – one hundred percent fair.'

'So, what are you going to do about it?' demanded Selkirk.

'Well, nothing, of course,' said the King.

'Nothing? Nothing!? You'll need to do a lot better than that!'

The King thought about it for a moment.

'Okay,' said the King. 'How about a re-run of the race? The same rules as always, but this time, like the very first race, the island is the prize.'

Selkirk turned to Cara and smiled. Just what they had hoped for, he thought.

'Okay, you're on,' said Selkirk. 'When?'

The King, now looking extremely flustered, said, 'How about next Saturday, when the sun is at its highest?'

'That doesn't give us much time,' whispered Cara to Selkirk.

'Just enough,' whispered Selkirk back.

'Okay,' said Selkirk. 'Next Saturday it is. Olly will referee. Agreed?'

'Agreed,' said the King.

Selkirk, Cara and all the rest of the animals and birds triumphantly marched back onto the beach and onwards to the causeway.

Back on the mainland, Cara and Selkirk sat down on the edge of the beach with Mikey, Benny, Henry, Olly and King Markus Theodore. Robin sat next to Selkirk.

Cara was first to speak.

'Mikey needs some training,' she said. 'With Maggie still injured, it's down to you, Mikey.'

'I know,' said Mikey nervously.

'If only Micah the Meteor was still around,' said Benny.

'He's long gone,' said Selkirk.

Olly suddenly piped up with his bombshell.

'He's still alive!' he said.

Chapter 13

Olly's bombshell

They all looked at Olly.

'Are you serious?' said Selkirk. 'He's really still alive?'

'Yes, very much so,' said Olly.

'Why didn't you say something?' asked Mikey.

'Nobody asked me,' said Olly. 'And anyway, he really didn't want anyone to know. As you all know, he blamed himself all those years ago for losing the race and letting Selkirk's great-grandfather down. They were very good friends. He just couldn't live with the shame, so he decided to fly away, never to return!'

'So where exactly is he?' asked Cara.

'He lives all alone now, like a hermit, up on the very top of Largo Law,' said Olly.

'He didn't get very far then,' chirped Mikey.

'He didn't want to leave the bay completely,' said Olly. 'Just far enough away so that he couldn't be a part of our family anymore. He was, in a way, punishing himself.'

'That is so sad,' said Cara.

And then Cara had an idea.

'I have an idea!' she shouted.

'Oh no!' said Selkirk. 'Here we go again.'

'Hey!' said Benny to Selkirk. 'Ease up on those negative vibes, man! So, what's the idea, Cara?'

'Well,' said Cara, 'as we all know, we have very little time. And we MUST win the race! Mikey is our only hope, but he needs more training. Even Mikey would admit to that!'

Mikey nodded in agreement.

'So,' said Cara, 'who do you think might be best to train Mikey?'

She left that last sentence hanging in the air. It was obvious, wasn't it?

Olly then piped up: 'Who?'

Cara looked over at Olly. 'You are kidding me, aren't you? Obviously' – she gave Olly a hard stare – 'it has to be Micah!'

'Of course,' said Mikey. 'He was the best flier in the bay after all.'

'Slow down there, amigos,' interrupted Benny. 'Let's not forget, Micah must be at least a hundred and fifty-two by now! What are the chances he'll even agree, never mind still be able to cut it?'

'Well first of all, he's not that old,' said Olly. 'He is a bit grumpy though ...'

'He's our only chance,' said Cara.

Selkirk agreed.

'What time is it?' said Cara.

Selkirk looked up at the sun.

'I'd say, about half past one.'

'Okay,' said Cara. 'That leaves me one and a half hours, I need to be home by three o'clock as my cousin Ellie is coming to visit. We need to get up there fast. Anyone got any ideas how we do that?'

Henry the Heron, who was standing quietly at the back, suddenly uncoiled his long neck.

'We'll all fly up!' he said.

'WHAT?' shouted Selkirk. 'Have you completely lost your mind?'

'Actually,' said Cara, 'that's not a bad idea.'

'Are you serious?' said Selkirk.

Chapter 14

The flight

'Pay no attention to Selkirk,' said Cara to Henry. 'What's the plan?'

'Well,' began Henry, 'it's really quite simple. My wife, Henrietta and I will lift you up by your arms and fly you up to the top of Largo Law. My nephew Hamish, will lift Selkirk. Mikey can lead the way.'

'Have you gone stark raving mad?' said Selkirk. 'You're a lunatic, it can't possibly work! You'll drop us for sure! We'll—'

Henry let out two loud squawks. From the nearby trees, Hamish and Henrietta swooped down.

'What is it, dear?' asked Henrietta.

Henry quickly told Henrietta of his plan to get Cara and Selkirk to the top of Largo Law.

'Great plan, Uncle Henry,' said Hamish.

Hamish then took hold of Selkirk and, grabbing each of his ears with his big claws, started to lift him skywards!

Selkirk shrieked as he was lifted higher and higher.

Down below, it was Cara's turn. She raised her arms above her head and Henry and Henrietta lifted her off the ground.

Cara started to laugh. 'I'm flying!' she shouted.

Back on the beach stood Benny. He was carrying Cara's little pink basket. Cara had asked him to get her shells as she wouldn't have time and didn't want to tell her dad another fib!

As Benny searched the beach for the right shells, Felix suddenly appeared.

'Hey, my friend!' said Felix. 'That's a lovely pink basket you've got there.'

'Are you making fun of me?' said Benny.

'Oh no, I wouldn't do that. WOULD I?' he said, and gestured towards the trees.

Benny looked over as another dozen foxes came out from behind the trees. They were all rolling about laughing!

Meanwhile, high above, Cara looked over at Selkirk. The sweat was pouring from his forehead and down to his little nose.

Cara chuckled as Selkirk grimaced and shouted, 'We're all going to die!'

They flew over Cara's back garden. Her dad was out mowing the lawn. He walked up and down with great purpose, never once looking up …

Onwards and upwards they flew. Closer and closer to the hill known as Largo Law.

In just a few short minutes they had arrived. Henry, Henrietta and Hamish landed them safely on the soft grass at the top of the law.

Selkirk threw himself onto the ground and kissed the grass!

'Happy now?' said Cara.

'Ecstatic!' said Selkirk.

'Well, when you've finished kissing the ground, we still need to walk up there,' Cara said, pointing to a large silver birch at the top of the hill.

Selkirk picked himself up off the grass and they started walking.

As they approached the tree, down swooped Micah the Meteor, landing right in front of them.

Chapter 15

Micah the Meteor

'What is the meaning of this intrusion?' Micah demanded.

'Hello, sir,' said Selkirk. 'My name is Selkirk McRabbie the Eighth. My great-grandfather was Selkirk McRabbie the Fifth.'

'Ah yes,' said Micah, 'I knew him well. He was a great rabbit and a good friend. But that was many years ago. Why have you come here now, disturbing my peace?'

'I can only apologise, sir, for intruding like this. However, we need your help.'

'We need you to train Mikey,' said Cara.

'And who are you?' said Micah.

'My name is Cara and we could really do with your expertise,' she said.

'I see.'

Selkirk piped up again.

'You may have heard about yesterday's race?' he said.

'Indeed I have,' said Micah, looking over at Mikey. 'I watched yesterday's race from up here. You, young magpie, have a lot to learn.'

'Will you train me?' asked Mikey of the old magpie.

Micah lowered his old and weary head.

'I'm afraid, son, I'm too old for that now. You see, I'm to blame for the loss of the island to the gulls. I vowed never to leave here for the shame of it.'

'It's not true,' said Selkirk. 'We found the proof on the island!'

Selkirk told the whole story to Micah, including how they managed to arrange a re-run of the race this coming Saturday.

Micah was flabbergasted.

'You mean it wasn't my fault after all?' He was almost in tears.

'No,' said Selkirk. 'The gulls fixed the race!'

'So, will you help us now?' Cara asked.

Micah looked up at the sky above and said, 'Of course I will. I owe it to Selkirk, to your great-grandfather. Let us win the island back together!'

Selkirk pumped the air with his fist.

'Yes!' he shouted.

Cara gave Micah a hug. Micah blushed.

'Now then, young magpie,' he said, looking over at Mikey. 'We have a lot to do and not much time to do it in! We start tomorrow. I'll fly down to the beach first thing in the morning. When the sun comes up, I want YOU up!'

'Yes, sir!' said Mikey.

Chapter 16

'Believe'

The return journey from Largo Law was just as much fun for Cara as the flight over – Selkirk screaming in terror and Cara laughing as if they were on a rollercoaster ride.

Dad was still in the garden and still not looking up. Now he was tending to his prize roses.

Henry and Henrietta dipped sideways on a gust of wind and their human cargo let out a little shriek.

Cara's dad looked up! He put his hand up to shield his eyes from the sun, and scanned to left and right, but the fliers had passed behind a row of trees.

Shaking his head, he returned to his roses.

Cara landed first, right where they had taken off, beside the great oak tree.

Above her, Selkirk was kicking his legs in all directions and shouting, 'Land! LAND!'

This time, he threw himself onto the sand and kissed it – a bad idea, as in doing so he swallowed some sand.

'W-water! WATER!' he spluttered. 'Can someone get me some water?'

Cara was in fits. 'That was brilliant fun!' she said. 'We need to do that again!'

'No chance!' said Selkirk, spitting out sand. 'I'd rather be thrown into a snake pit!'

'Well, anyway', said Cara, 'mission accomplished!'

'Indeed,' said Selkirk. 'Now it's over to you, Mikey!'

'Look, guys,' said Mikey, 'I'm not sure I can do this. I mean, you all saw what happened in the first race. I blew it!'

'Don't be so silly,' said Cara. 'Of course you can do it. Micah has agreed to train you now. Everything will be just fine.'

'That's easy for you to say. You're not the one getting up at the crack of dawn tomorrow!'

Just then, King Markus Theodore flew down from the great oak tree.

'I heard what you said, Mikey,' he said. 'Don't worry son, we're all behind you. You can do it!'

Then Benny piped up. 'Hey, man, you'll blow these cats out of the air. I believe in you!'

'You see?' said Cara. 'You've got to *believe*, Mikey! Repeat after me: I'm Mikey Magpie, I'm the greatest flier of all time and I'm going to WIN!'

'Say it!' she repeated.

'Okay,' said Mikey. 'I'm Mikey Magpie, I'm the greatest flier of all time and I'm going to WIN!'

'Again.'

'I'm Mikey Magpie, I'm the greatest flier of all time and I'm going to WIN!'

Everyone cheered!

'It must be nearly three o'clock,' said Cara. 'I need to get home. Cousin Ellie will be there any minute.'

Selkirk said, 'See you tomorrow?'

'Of course,' said Cara. 'I may bring along Ellie, if that's okay?'

'Yeah, doll face, that would be coolio,' said Benny.

'I think you'll find, Benny, that Cara was speaking to me.' Selkirk turned to Cara. 'Of course. That's fine,' he said.

'Great!' said Cara. 'Good luck with the training, Mikey. See you all tomorrow then.' And she ran back home.

Chapter 17

Ellie

As Cara ran into the house by the back door, Ellie was coming in the front.

Perfect timing, thought Cara.

The two cousins hugged. They hadn't seen each other for a few months. It wasn't very often that Ellie managed to come over as she lived so far away, in Glasgow.

'Can you help Ellie upstairs with her stuff Cara, please?' asked Dad.

Cara grabbed Ellie's bag and they both ran off upstairs.

'I've got so much to tell you!' said Cara. 'You won't believe what has been going on around here, these last couple of days.'

She told Ellie the whole story.

When Cara had finished, Ellie took a deep breath and said, 'Wow! This *is* unbelievable! Have you told your dad?'

'Absolutely not,' said Cara. 'He wouldn't believe a word of it. In fact, he must not find out. It's our secret, right?!'

'Right!'

'I asked if I could bring you along tomorrow,' said Cara. 'Selkirk said it would be okay.'

'Brilliant! I can't wait!'

As per usual, the next morning the cockerel screamed out its now customary wake-up call.

'Does that happen every morning?' asked Ellie.

'Yup!' said Cara, hiding under her pillow. 'Same time every single morning.'

'Well, at least you don't need to buy an alarm clock!'

Just then, Cara's dad shouted through the door. 'You guys up?'

'Did you not hear the cockerel?' shouted Cara.

'Take your point,' said Dad, chuckling. 'Breakfast?'

'You bet!'

'Well, get up then! I'm making bacon rolls.'

Cara and Ellie shot up!

When they got downstairs, Dad was dishing up the bacon rolls.

'So, what's the plan today?' he asked.

Cara looked at Ellie and winked.

'I think we'll just go for a walk along the beach this morning, Dad.'

Ellie smiled.

'Sounds like a good idea,' said Dad. 'It's a lovely day out there.'

After breakfast, Cara and Ellie went back upstairs to get ready. When they came down, they found Dad looking out the window.

'What is it?' asked Cara.

'Well, I could have sworn I berthed the dinghy in a different place to where it is now.'

'Oops,' said Cara under her breath.

'You wouldn't know anything about that, would you Cara?'

'I think your mind is playing tricks on you Dad. It must be your age ...' She chuckled.

'Cheeky.'

'Okay, we're off,' said Cara. 'We'll be back for lunch.'

'See you later then. And no messing about. Have a good time girls.'

Cara and Ellie raced down to the beach and along to the great oak tree.

Chapter 18

Training

There was not a soul around when they reached the oak tree.

Cara looked around. Nothing!

'Are you sure you didn't just imagine all this, Cara?' said Ellie.

'Of course not.'

All of a sudden, Selkirk bounced out from behind the oak tree.

'BOO!' he shouted.

'Look,' said Cara, 'it wasn't funny the first time and it sure isn't funny this time!'

'A thousand apologies,' said Selkirk. 'But she actually did thin it was funny!' He turned to Ellie. 'You must be Ellie, Cara's cousin,' he said, holding out his hand.

Ellie shook Selkirk's hand.

'Pleased to meet you,' she said.

'So, Selkirk,' said Cara, 'what's been happening? How is Mikey getting on with his training?'

'Well, funny you should ask. Do you recall that Micah had ordered Mikey to be down here this morning when the sun was just rising?'

'Yes.'

'Well, it turns out Micah slept in! Mikey was sat down here waiting for him for two hours! You couldn't make it up!' He laughed.

'I don't suppose Mikey would have been very pleased about that ...' said Cara.

'Absolutely not. But he certainly wasn't going to say anything to the great Micah 'The Meteor' Magpie, was he? So, when Micah finally arrived, they just got on with it.'

'Where are they now?'

Selkirk looked skywards.

Cara and Ellie both looked up.

They could see Micah barking out orders to Mikey as he approached the great oak tree at high speed.

'Wings back!' boomed Micah. 'Feet up! You're coming in too fast! Slow down! SLOW DOWN!'

Mikey slammed straight into a large branch and summersaulted onto the face of the trunk. Then he slid all the way down to the bottom, hitting more branches before finally landing at the feet of Selkirk.

'Not bad, not bad,' mocked Selkirk. 'Seven!' he shouted, holding up a scorecard and laughing at his own joke.

'That's not helping!' said Mikey. 'Since when were you an expert on flying anyway? As I recall, you didn't much enjoy your own time in the air yesterday!'

Selkirk's laughter suddenly subsided.

'I ... I ... don't think that's anything to do..'

'Ha!' said Mikey.

Micah then flew down. He stood over the slumped body of Mikey.

'Well done, son' he said, to the complete surprise of all around. 'Much better!'

Ellie turned to Cara and whispered, 'If that was much better, I'd hate to see his previous attempts'

'Fear not!' said Micah. 'Practice makes perfect! Now, do it again.'

Mikey scraped himself off the trunk of the tree, dusted himself down and flew off, readying himself for another attempt.

'Do you think he'll be ready?' asked Cara.

'Don't worry, Cara,' said Micah. 'He'll be fine. I'm just getting started!'

Selkirk frowned.

'Okay, we'll leave you to it,' said Cara.

Micah flew off into the sky in the direction of Mikey.

Selkirk bounced over. 'This doesn't look good,' he said.

'Don't worry,' said Cara. 'He's going to get better.'

'How do you know?'

'The determination in his eyes,' she said. 'He believes! And I believe too!'

Cara and Ellie went back to the house and Cara helped Ellie pack. When it was time for Ellie to leave, they hugged, and Ellie made Cara promise to tell her all about the race.

For the rest of the week, Cara had to go to school. She took the shells with her and finished her project, and the teacher gave her an A. Top marks! Her dad was very proud.

Every day after school, Cara went down to the beach to see the progress Mikey was making.

He was getting better and better, but he needed more time.

Friday came too fast. Tomorrow was the day of the big race.

That night, Cara tossed and turned, dreaming of a glorious victory ...

Chapter 19

'We're doomed!'

It was Saturday morning, the day of the race.

Cara awoke to the sunshine streaming through the gap in the curtains.

She stretched out her arms and legs and let out a long and very satisfying yawn.

'This is the day!' she said, and looked at her clock. 8:15.

How strange, she thought. *No cockerel. Where was my ridiculously, far too early and extremely irritating wake-up call?*

Was it a bad sign? Was there something wrong? Could this day end badly? No! she told herself. This was going to be a glorious day!

After breakfast, Cara put on her lucky blue top. She had worn it only twice before. At last year's school sports day, when she had won the egg and spoon race, and also on the day she was given an A for her school project.

'What can go wrong,' she said to herself.

She bounded down the stairs and into the living room. Dad was listening to the news on the radio.

'Morning, Cara.'

'Morning.'

'Have you seen outside yet?' said Dad.

'Yup. It's absolutely glorious. There isn't a cloud in the sky. It's going to be a great day!'

'What do you have planned then?'

'Oh, nothing much,' said Cara, and smiled. 'Think I'll go down to the beach for a while.'

'Okay. Have Fun!'

Fingers crossed, thought Cara, and she rushed out of the house and down the steps to the beach.

When Cara arrived at the great oak tree, a large crowd had already gathered. All were trying to find the best position from which to watch the race.

Selkirk stood at the side of the great oak tree. He had a big beaming smile from ear to ear.

'So, what do you think of our chances?' said Cara.

Selkirk thought about it for a second, but before he had a chance to answer, down swooped Micah.

'Let's see what Micah thinks,' said Selkirk. 'What are Mikey's chances, Micah?'

'Well, he has done well in training,' said Micah.

'Excellent!' said Selkirk. 'How are his turns and landings?'

'His landings are atrocious and his turns are even worse!' said Micah.

'WHAT! How is he going to win if he can't land or turn? I don't believe it. We're doomed,' he said, and groaned.

Micah looked hard at Selkirk. 'You're just like your old great-grandfather Selkirk, you know. The cup is always half-empty, never half-full. Benny was right. You give off too many negative vibes. Calm down. Mikey has it covered. I've taught him a few new skills.'

'Well, I hope you're right, Micah,' said Selkirk.

Above them, King Markus Theodore the Third stood on one of the great oak tree's highest branches.

Chapter 20

The Race for Home

Cara looked all around. Everyone was there.

Benny and his pal Felix were sitting on a rock just down the beach. Henrietta and Hamish stood together on the sand. Robin sat next to Selkirk.

Sitting on a rock at the foot of the great oak was Colin, the cockerel.

So, there you are, thought Cara.

Over on the island, Mikey and Angus stood side by side, with King Steven and his queen perched on a tree behind them.

In the sky, circling the hill, was Olly, ready to referee.

Henry had also taken up his position, on the rock on the island foreshore.

There was a hush all around.

The big, booming voice of King Markus Theodore the Third shattered the silence.

'I, King Markus Theodore the Third, ruler of all Amazonia, do hereby declare that this, the second great race for Selkirk's Island, may now commence!'

Henry gave his usual high-pitched squawk and the race began.

Off they went!

Once again, Mikey got off to a good start.

Hard on his tail feathers flew Angus.

They were going at breakneck speed around the island. It was hard for Olly to keep up with them.

They were both on their way across the bay now, heading towards the great oak tree.

Mikey had fallen slightly behind Angus but was coming back at him.

As they approached the great oak, Selkirk covered his face with both hands, but he could just about peak out and he saw Mikey pass Angus and swoop down towards the top of the tree.

They all looked up. This was the big moment. Could Mikey get his twig without crashing into the trunk?

Mikey dived and without even stopping, scooped up his twig and flew off as fast as he could, heading to the old railway bridge.

Micah looked over at Selkirk with a told-you-so look.

Right behind Mikey, and tearing through the sky like a dart, was Angus, who had also picked up his twig with ease. Determined as ever, he flew faster and faster.

The approach to the bridge was tricky, as they had to fly through some big pine trees.

Mikey made it through first, but only just.

Angus appeared to find another gear and raced past Mikey.

Down below, the whole crowd groaned.

'C'mon Mikey!' shouted Cara.

Under the bridge flew Angus and, with a beautifully executed turn, was on his way back, disappearing on the other side of the bridge for a moment.

'This was always going to be a disaster,' said Selkirk. 'He can't turn …'

Just then, Mikey did something that no one expected. No one, that is, except Micah.

He went into a loop the loop manoeuvre and passed over the bridge completely upside down, righting himself as he emerged and going faster than he had ever flown!

Now he was right on Angus's tail feathers.

They were neck and neck flying over the harbour and out to sea, over the bay towards the island.

Then, just as they crossed over the shoreline, Mikey slowed himself down a little.

'What is he doing?' shouted Selkirk.

'Don't worry,' said Micah.

Angus was getting ready to dive towards the basket and drop his twig in, while above him Mikey had already dropped his twig!

There wasn't a sound as the twig floated down. It drifted sideways a little, but Mikey had allowed for the breeze. Just as Angus was about to drop his twig gently into the basket, Mikey's twig flashed across his line of vision and landed in the basket with a satisfying thwack!

A huge roar went up!

Mikey had done it! He had won the race but, more importantly, with the help and support of all of his friends he had won the island back!

The tears that Selkirk had been holding back were now rolling down his cheeks. Tears of happiness as he hugged Robin.

Everyone was shouting and screaming for joy!

Cara hugged Micah. Felix hugged Benny. And Henrietta kissed Henry!

King Steven flew across the water from the island and landed right in front of Selkirk.

'It would seem you have won,' said the King and he lowered his head, graciously accepting defeat.

Selkirk stood up tall.

'Thank you,' he said to the King. 'Angus did you proud!'

'Mikey also,' the King said.

'I've been thinking,' said Selkirk. 'The island is quite big. There is more than enough room over there for all of us.'

'What are you saying?' asked the King.

'I'm saying, you don't have to leave. We can all live there together, in peace.'

'You are a fine young rabbit, Selkirk,' said the King. 'On behalf of my flock, I accept your kind offer. Tonight, we must all have a party to celebrate!'

'Absolutely!' said Selkirk.

Cara was sitting on the shingle with her back against the great oak tree.

All's well that ends well, she thought.

Selkirk walked across to where Cara was sitting.

'I don't know how to thank you,' said Selkirk. 'You have helped me – and all of us – so much. If it wasn't for you, nothing would have changed here. I owe you the earth.'

'Don't be silly, Selkirk. I was happy to do it for you, and you know why?'

'Why?' said Selkirk.

'Because,' said Cara, 'you are my friend.'

Cara stood up and gave Selkirk a big hug. Then she waved to everyone before heading back along the beach towards the house.

'What a day it has been,' said Cara to herself as she sat on the garden bench a little later.

She gazed in the fading light towards the island, and it sounded like the party had already begun.

Her dad's binoculars were on her lap, and used them to take a closer look. She could swear she saw Selkirk and Robin dancing. Gulls and magpies were squawking together and everyone was having a great time.

'It's certainly been an interesting couple of weeks,' she said as she climbed the steps to the front door. 'I wonder what will happen next ...'

She closed the door behind her and headed up the stairs to her bedroom.

'Can't *wait* to tell Ellie!'

Chapter 21

The old lady

The old lady looked at Emma, Paul and their parents over the rim of her glasses and said:

'And that was that.'

'Wow!' said Emma.

'That was a brilliant story!' said Paul. 'You're such a good storyteller!'

'Was it true?' asked Emma.

'Of course my dear, every word,' said the old lady.

'Well, that certainly was an interesting tale,' said Michael as he stood up.

Suzanne stretched out her hand. 'Thank you very much for your time,' she said. 'I'm sure we'll see you again when we move in next month.'

'I'm sure you will, dear,' said the old lady.

'Come along children,' said Suzanne.

As they walked towards the steps to the beach, Suzanne turned back.

'I'm sorry, we didn't get your name?' she said.

'Oh,' said the old lady, 'It's Mrs Stuart.'

'Thank you, Mrs Stuart,' said Suzanne.

She disappeared into the house, closing the door behind her.

The old lady went into her living room and walked through towards the kitchen.

'I hope you didn't tell them everything,' said a voice from behind her.

The old lady turned around.

'Of course I didn't,' she said.

'Just as well,' said Selkirk. He was sitting on the sofa, watching the television. 'I have the strangest feeling they might not have believed you. Are you making a cup of tea, Cara?'

'Yes, good idea. Would you like some?'

'Yes please, said Selkirk.

'Oh, and do you have any carrots?'

Cara smiled...

THE END

About the Author:

Michael Stuart, originally from Edinburgh, now living in the small coastal village of Lower Largo in Fife, Scotland. He lives there with his wife Suzanne and their golden retriever, Holly. This is his first book, however there are more in the pipeline. Michael can be contacted directly via his e-mail address: mas7166@btinternet.com or via his Facebook page - @mykoolbooks

Printed in Poland
by Amazon Fulfillment
Poland Sp. z o.o., Wrocław